T0208426

I Know You Will Make It

Safford Chamberlain

iUniverse, Inc.

New York Bloomington

I Know You Will Make It

Copyright © 2009 by Safford Chamberlain

iUniverse books may be ordered through booksellers or by contacting:
iUniverse
1663 Liberty Drive
Bloomington, IN 47403
www.iuniverse.com
1-800-Authors (1-800-288-4677)

Because of the dynamic nature of the Internet, any Web addresses or links contained in this book may have changed since publication and may no longer be valid. This is a work of fiction. All of the characters, names, incidents, organizations, and dialogue in this novel are either the products of the author's imagination or are used fictitiously.

ISBN: 978-1-4401-5730-1 (pbk)
ISBN: 978-1-4401-5731-8 (ebk)

Library of Congress Control Number: 2009931836

Printed in the United States of America
iUniverse rev. date: 7/31/2009

To my children,
Desiree Marie Chamberlain,
and Thornton Louis Chamberlain,
and to my dear wife, Sharyn Crane,
whose love has sustained me

Once out of nature I shall never take

My bodily form from any natural thing,

But such a form as Grecian goldsmiths make

Of hammered gold and gold enamelling

To keep a drowsy emperor awake;

Or set upon a golden bough to sing

To lords and ladies of Byzantium

Of what is past, or passing, or to come.

from "Sailing to Byzantium" by William Butler Yeats

CONTENTS

PREFACE

With one exception, all of these stories were written after 1980, when I turned 54. The exception is the title story, *I Know You Will Make It*, which was first written in 1954 for my Masters thesis at Cornell University. Much revised since then, it is set in Berkeley, California, where I was living at that time. Like all of my stories, it is grounded in my own experience, in this case the breakup of my first marriage, which lasted only five months. The autobiographical germ of *Lester and Billie Jean* was a rejection by a girl in my first year of high school, plus my experience in middle age of learning to play jazz saxophone. The *Lester* of the title is the great jazz saxophonist Lester Young, who is also the subject of one of my poems. The plot of *The Skinhead Gig* is wholly fictional, although of course it grew out of my jazz experience. *Homecoming* draws upon my experience in the army at the end of World War II. *Higher Education* is about a conflict with my father.

I KNOW YOU WILL MAKE IT

Yesterday I got up early, took a shower, swallowed the sun like a pill, and took the F-train to the city. At the United Press office the bureau chief and I talked Faulkner for awhile. He offered me a shot of Jack Daniels, which I accepted, but they still hadn't any openings. In fact, he said, they never would. UP was going under, Associated Press had stolen the day away, and in six months he, the bureau chief, would probably be writing press releases for some goddam corporation, Ford or General Electric or whatever.

I still couldn't bring myself to check out the *Examiner.* I stayed away from the Hearst papers because I couldn't stand their red-baiting McCarthyist politics. I learned my politics, such as they are, from my Dad, who taught classes in socialism before he became a Roosevelt New Dealer. He's backslid a little since then. Now he's a Truman Democrat, thinks the Korean war is necessary, a police action, the civilized West against the Commie hordes. Maybe he's right. Except it wasn't the Communists that dropped atomic bombs on Hiroshima and Nagasaki. For that matter it wasn't the Commies that invented the Inquisition in the name of Christ, or wiped out the American Indians in the name of Manifest Destiny. Don't get me wrong, Truman's atom bombs saved my ass. Instead of being blown up as an infantry replacement in an invasion of Japan, here I am, an unemployed master of arts with a cuckold's horns on his head, alas.

At the California Newspaper Publishers Association the only job they had was in Calexico. I didn't think I would mind living in Calexico for a year, except I've moved around quite a bit in the last few years, and I'm sick of it. Also, I think I may be just a tad neurotic. Ha ha. I'm totally fucked up. So if I ever get some money I'd like to have my head shrunk a little, and I doubt if they have a psychoanalyst in Calexico. An abortionist or two, probably, but unfortunately my wife dumped me, and my sex life does not give rise to that kind of need just now.

On the way across the bay bridge I decided to take a bus out to the Oakland canneries. Nothing doing, they said, till mid-summer.

When I got back to my room in Berkeley there was a letter from Hilton. I propped myself up on the bed with pillows and settled down to read Hilton's letter:

"Myron: I have done it. Eleanor's departure has driven me from wrack to wruin. Pot and soul-syrup are my undoing. To make it short though not sweet, I am busted. I daresay my parents are suffering agonies of soul-searching, wondering what they did to produce a son so sunk in iniquity. Although, indeed, it could be viewed as something less than doomsday. First offense, just holding, and all that. I expect the Army will gladly rescue me from the embarrassment of jail, as bodies are still in demand in Korea. So, my good and faithful friend, Fate steps most definitively between us. Be good to yourself. I do not understand. The horror, the horror."

I lay there, taking it in. Trying less to sweeten life than to stand it, Hilton was now a crook, a dope fiend, a moral degenerate. Hilton, one of the world's last living gentlemen. With his tight-curled blondish hair, his sappy, dashing good looks, and his baroque Samuel Johnson lingo, he was the incarnation of that old comic strip defender of the working girl's honor, Hairbreadth Harry. Once at a party he actually butted into a fight between a guy and his girl with, "Indeed, sir, you shall not touch her." Completely broke the guy's rhythm. Of course it helped that Hilton is six foot three.

Now he was busted. Even if you couldn't swallow cops as conscience, your parents could, and did. Hilton left grad school, he claimed, because he was using his parents' money under false pretenses. They imagined he would get his doctorate and join the comfortable ranks of paid academia, whereas he was merely indulging himself in "the gentlemanly pursuit of literature." It offended his conception of the profession of belles lettres to think that he had to have union card, i.e. a Ph.D., to do it.

At least that's what he said. The real reason he left Berkeley was that Eleanor took that fellowship in France, and he couldn't stand Berkeley anymore. So he went home to L.A. to wait for the draft.

Too bad the army hadn't got him sooner. I could imagine what it would be like if my parents had to bail me out on a narcotics charge. As Hilton said, they would think it was their fault. My mother might remember, with tears in her eyes, how she spanked me for stealing from her penny collection or scolded me for walking in the rain to try out my new raincoat. I don't know what my Dad would remember, he's such a loving man. But he'd find something, and that abstracted, pained look would grave itself deeper into the corners of his eyes, he would have one more piece of dross to convert, somehow, back to original gold. What it is, I'm his prodigal son, all my failures are forgiven in advance. That's what makes failing so dreadful.

Like I failed with Betty. Or Betty failed with me. Or the universe failed when it didn't go into convulsions and blast that scrawny little bastard Herbie off the face of the earth with one outraged thunderbolt. That it felt no outrage was a fact I had difficulty living with. I know, of course, that it was at least as much me as either of them. Over the two years of our love affair I had given her plenty of reasons, I'm sure, to break it off. But I try hard not to hate myself, and I can't hate Betty because I want her too much. Also, I've always known she was borderline crazy, not totally in control. My Dad called her a slut. He knew better. She's not a slut. Hating Herbie is the best I can do.

Yet none of it is fun to think about, so when the movie-camera images started--my all-night girlie-bar binge, coming home to an empty apartment next morning, getting loaded and walking clear to Richmond, stopping at every bar to call home, finding out that night that she was at Herbie's in North Beach, standing over both of them on his ratty couch, me on the edge of grabbing him and bashing him against the wall, which I could have done, he's so puny--when the brain camera started grinding out the images, I got up and rolled a couple of extra-fat joints. But the fact was I had not been enjoying the stuff so much lately. I would start by feeling guilty about what I had done to my mind; maybe I would try to talk to somebody and keep forgetting the beginnings of my sentences; then I would quit talking, but if a bad thought came to me, like Betty saying no, she wouldn't come home, she was with Herbie now, I wouldn't be able to get rid of it, it would just take over.

I considered the consequences of quitting: endless days and nights of facing not as little as possible but as much as there was. Then I would need a job, not the temporary clerk-typist jobs I'd been surviving on but something I could do and feel good about doing. That provision eliminated practically everything but newspaper work, but even with a year's experience and a scrapbook full of clippings, I wasn't much more than a beginner, and you had to have some pull just to get on as a copy boy. The only other possibility was teaching English, but I'd have to go back to school to get a state teaching credential. And naturally I would want to make it with a woman, but for some reason I could not seem to meet one who wasn't a transparent idiot compared to Betty. But suppose I could: what evidence was there that I could do any better with a new woman than with Betty?

But OK, I could wait. I could try clear-headedness, for an evening, at least. I put on the windbreaker Betty bought me in L.A., stuffed Hilton's letter in my pocket, and set out for Victor's, where my new friends liked to congregate. I had had to find new friends because my old friends in Berkeley were all friends of Herbie's.

At Victor's the plate glass door pushed against my palm like a warning. Kay's busty profile floated up through the yellow atmosphere, plump and animated, talking to her leftist friends, and further up the narrow aisle, fuzzy in the gloom of the hindmost recesses, sat Larry and Smitty and Norman. Larry, the biggest pothead of us all, was also a serious classical bassoonist, a music major who practiced three and four hours a day. Smitty was a town kid dropout who had picked up on jazzers like Lennie Tristano and his star students Warne Marsh and Lee Konitz and who played pretty good piano, not Tristano-ish by a long shot, but not corny either. Norman was another town guy, a cool black guy in his mid-twenties who sounded like his idol, Buck Clayton.

I set my eyes straight ahead and went into my Victor's walk, leaning forward as if with purpose. As I had hoped, I made it past Kay without her noticing. There was too much of Kay. Her breasts were monuments, like those of the proletarian women in communist murals. They were a bribe, a promise of plenitude at which one could suck forever, vaguely repulsive because she used them to get things from you. Which of course she couldn't do if you didn't let her.

Pallid, slack-mouthed, acquiline of nose, Larry was saying something about Bird, Charlie Parker, our great culture hero. He stopped as I sat down beside Norman, who put his trumpet case on his lap to give me room.

"Don't stop," I said. "What about Bird?"

"I dreamed about him, man."

"Screw Bird," said Smitty. "He's been goofing for fifteen minutes trying to tell us. Why don't you turn us all on, man?"

Smitty was at his spookiest, his body crouched and his head tilted back, the eyes giving the effect of being crossed while staring straight ahead.

"You talk too loud," said Larry, staring back.

"How about the dream," I said.

Larry closed his eyes and began to tell it.

"I went to this session. Bird was sitting here, right out in the aisle, blowing my bassoon. It was his birthday party, and he was blowing these terrible sounds, playing like a kid who didn't know anything. Dying snakes, man, that's what he sounded like. It didn't make any sense to anyone, they thought he was putting them on."

Kay came over from the other table. She gave my hand a squeeze and laid her books on the table. One was *The Unconscious,* the text for a course she was taking. She was studying to be a psychologist. The other was Trotsky's *History of the Russian Revolution,* which I still haven't read.

"So I said to him," Larry went on, "'Man, why don't you play your own horn? You're making a fool of yourself.' But he just kept blowing these terrible sounds. I wanted to stop him, but I couldn't move. Then everybody got mad at him. They yelled at him, 'Arrraaaaagh,' like the mob at the crucifixion. And then, man"--he fixed me with glazed, watery eyes--"I looked down at myself, and I realized I was naked, and Bird was naked too, dumpy and black and naked. And they made us leave. It was Bird's birthday party, and they threw him out. Bird was juiced on their liquor, and when they threw us out, he fell down and couldn't get up. 'Help,' he said, and he was laughing, 'Help, man, I can't get up.' It was a big joke to him. I began to laugh too, and then I was crying. I was on my knees with my arms around Bird, and he was laughing and I was crying."

Kay cocked her head at him. "Is this supposed to be a real dream?"

Larry stared at her.

"Just asking," said Kay. "I don't suppose you want to know what it means."

"Oh man," groaned Larry. "Meet Miss Freud."

"It means Larry's queer," said Smitty, winking at Kay. "All that blowing on horns, all that eating."

"It doesn't have anything to do with homosexuality," said Kay. "Not in a specific sense. Does it, Larry?"

"Go away," said Larry. "I know what it means. Want me to tell you what it means? It means go fuck yourself. It means whuuummmmm. WHUUUUMMMMMMM!"

"Very good, " said Kay. "Now tell me what this means: a guy playing horrible sounds on your bassoon gets thrown out of his own birthday party for being naked, falls down from drinkiing their liquor, and says

'Help.' Pretty obvious, huh?"

"Whuuuummmmmm," said Larry. "Whuuuum-mmmmmm."

"What's the matter with you guys? How does a person eat and drink at his actual birthday?"

"I got it, Teach," said Smitty. "At Mommy's sweet titty. Mmmmmm-mmm. And that's why you're queer, man. An intellectual told me. Queers get hung on sucking Mommy's titties."

Norman started laughing. "I must be queer too, man. I'm hung on that too. So are you, man." He and Smitty fell out laughing.

"Aw, shit," said Larry, burying his face in his hands.

"I told you what you should do," said Smitty. "It's not my fault I'm not attuned to you."

"Am I attuned to you, Myron?" Kay rubbed her cheek against my arm and slid her hand into the pocket of my jacket, trying to twine her fingers in mine. I was holding on to Hilton's letter.

"What have you got in there?" She pulled at my hand.

"It's a letter," I said, bringing it out. "From a friend of ours you didn't know." I passed the letter to Larry.

11

"Hilton's busted."

"Christ," said Larry, reading it.

"Who's Hilton?" said Kay. "Do I get to touch the sacred relic?"

"It wouldn't mean anything to you," I said.

"God, you're exasperating! I'm asking you to tell me who he is so I can understand what it means!"

"She wants to be initiated," said Smitty, leering.

"Not possible," said Larry, handing the letter to Norman. "And sure as hell not by you. I don't know why I put up with you, man, just because you can play changes. I tell you a beautiful dream and you just laugh." He turned to me. "Let's leave these hack artists, man. I've got some stuff for you to try."

"What about me?" said Smitty. "What about Norman here?"

"I'm cool," said Norman. "You be cool too, okay?" He handed the letter to Smitty. "Try this for cool--'Pot and soul-syrup'--I like that. Make a sad song."

Larry got up to leave. Smitty got up too, the unread letter in his hand. "Sit down. Forget it, " said Larry. He turned to me. "You coming, man?"

"Thanks, man. I'm good."

Larry nodded, gave Smitty a glare, and slumped down the aisle to the door.

Kay patted my hand. "Good for you."

"Hey, man," said Smitty, "how about laying a couple of joints on me?"

I had known this was coming. He'd heard me tell Larry I was good.

"I've only got one," I lied.

"We can split it."

"No, man. You going to read the letter?"

He glowered. "Who gives a damn about Hilton? If he's busted, it's his own fault. Narcs everywhere."

"You want a beer?" I asked Kay. I was beginning to need one.

"No, but I'll watch you drink one."

I walked back to the counter. When I turned around with my mug of beer, I ran straight into Ted Green and Lorraine Willoughby. I had not seen Green since the night after Betty had first stayed with Herbie, when I went to get her and she had refused to come home. Green and others at Herbie's place had witnessed the whole rotten scene. I knew he had nothing to do with anything, but I had not talked to him since then. Now it was a shock seeing him with Lorraine. She was smiling at me in that sweet madonna way she had. I had slept with her a few times after Betty left, but it was no use. In bed together we were like ingeniously designed robots, making all the graceful passionate gestures but utterly incapable of feeling for each other. Yet she had a certain vestigial part in my fantasy life.

"How have you been?" I said.

"How have *you* been," said Green pointedly. "Haven't seen you around."

"Nor I," said Lorraine sweetly.

"I run with a different crowd now. Musicians. Stalinists."

Green had been at a party Betty and I attended where Herbie had held forth on how Miles Davis was a Stalinist because when he had played at the Downbeat Club he occasionally played into the back wall to hear himself better, turning his back to the audience. Green was a fringe member of Herbie's crowd of anti-Stalinist socialists.

Lorraine said, "We're having a party at my place Friday, if you want to come."

"No thanks," I said, remembering the New Year's Eve party, a few weeks after Betty left, that I had insanely gotten loaded and gone to, knowing that Herbie and Betty would be there. I was wearing my black overcoat and carrying in two hands a quart bottle of lousy Ten-High whisky. I walked by the people sitting on cushions in the living room, down the hall past the people in bedrooms, through the kitchen and past the people talking there, back through the living room, out the still open front door, and up the street.

Halfway up the block I had heard the missing engine of Herbie's pre-war Ford as it turned into the street at the other end. My friends, Betty and Herbie's friends, were calling to me. I kept walking. I walked the two miles home and drank the lousy Ten-High.

"I don't think so," I said. "There's probably a jam session I have to go to."

As I walked back to the table, Red Florence came through the door lugging his bass drum. There would be music soon. And not a moment too soon.

At the table Norman was unpacking his trumpet and Kay was talking to Smitty and one of her political friends, a hard-faced older guy, organizer type, probably a CPer, i.e. Stalinist. The House Un-American Activities Committee was going to hold hearings in the city in a few weeks, and Kay and her militant buddies were going to stand on the sidewalk and hand out leaflets.

"Why don't you come?" said Kay.

"Maybe. What do the leaflets say?"

"We haven't written them yet," said Hard-Face. "What do you think they should say?"

"How about 'Down with mean, greedy, selfish millionaires with little pig's eyes.' Or my personal favorite, 'Down with anti-Stalinist socialist shits who fuck their friends' wives.'"

"Legalize pot," said Smitty, not getting it.

"Legalize jazz," said Norman, laughing. "Bird for President."

"Be serious," said Kay.

"Okay," I said. "Here's a really great idea. All of us dress in black--black shirt, black pants, black overcoat, black homburg hats. We carry black umbrellas. We go into the hearing, we sit all in a row, we don't say a word, and right in the middle of it we all stand up, open our umbrellas, and march out."

"God," said Kay. "Whatever happened to politics?"

Hard-Face looked amused. "Interesting idea. A little indirect, but interesting."

"Right," I said. "You'll have to excuse me. It's hard to beat 'Death to the capitalist running dogs.'"

Twisting to watch Red carrying in his toms and cymbals, I got a little giddy and almost spilled my beer. Hard-Face got up to go. Norman started blowing soft long tones on his trumpet, warming up. *How did he do it,* I wondered. *How did a Negro like Norman stay so good-natured, so cool and serene?* It occurred to me there were advantages to being a Negro. If you couldn't get an decent job, if your wife ran out on you, if you loved to fuck up your mind with booze or dope, if you broke your parents' heart, if you just gave up on yourself, nobody cared, nobody expected you to do any better than shuffle around grinning and saying yassuh boss and feeling sorry for yourself. Except that Norman wasn't like that, I was.

I stood up.

"Where are you going? You haven't finished your beer," said Kay.

"I have to go."

"I'll wait for you. I want to talk to you."

Outside the fog had rolled in. At the paperback store on the corner I bought a pack of envelopes and a cheap tablet of lined writing paper. I put a dime in the stamp machine and got a four, a two, and a one, which was a gyp.

Back in the street I started walking down Channing Way. I didn't light up because Channing was the street Betty had lived on, in an airy attic apartment, the first time we separated, before we were married. I had come from L.A. to patch things up, which we half did, in a way that left me still aching.

When I got past her old place, I took out my joint and lit up. The high kicked in before I got back to Telegraph, and by the time I got to Victor's I was wailing, whaling, out of my head and happy again.

Kay and Smitty and Larry were at the table. Smitty looked sore about something, glaring at Larry. Some guy I didn't know was playing piano. Probably that was what Smitty was sore about, that and/or the fact that Larry wouldn't turn him on.

Kay squeezed my hand. The musicians were playing a ballad, "These Foolish Things." Oh how the ghost of you clings. My yes. I took out my pen and my writing pad. I stared at them for a minute, and then, because I couldn't think what to write to Hilton, I took out an envelope and began addressing it. Printing Hilton's name, I found I was making each letter differently, each expressing a different character. The "*H*" was solid, authoritatively righteous; the "*I*" was foolishly slanted and slightly bent, not as upright as it should be; the "*L*" had a quirky, untrustworthy foot; the "*T*" was full of barely suppressed rage; the "*O*" was lopsided, unsure of itself. The last letter, the "*N,*" was so hip I couldn't believe it. It knew all, yet was absolutely undaunted. I marveled. Then I started on Hilton's last name, Greenberg. This time I started very small and made each succeeding letter bigger. And suddenly it frightened and astounded me, this concept of time, of fate, of inevitability.

"Wow!" I said.

Kay put her hand on my arm. Then Smitty said something in a snarling voice that I didn't quite catch.

Larry said, "Sit down, you moron!"

But Smitty was already standing up, and I heard his voice, loud:

"Larry's holding! You hear that, narcs? Right here, Larry's your man!"

Smitty would not sit down. The sound seemed still to be coming out of his mouth. The musicians were still playing "These Foolish Things." I looked for the narcs. Two guys I knew to be football players looked at Smitty with narc-like expressions on their faces. They rose up and came down on us. I knew they didn't care about Smitty or Larry, it was me who had murdered his mind, and I was doubly guilty because my paents would think it was their fault. They walked right past Larry, not giving him even a look. They walked right past me, and I knew they weren't narcs at all, and that I had always known it. There was reality and there were narcs, and it was all just me. Everything was just itself. I looked around and saw that everyone, everything, was just being itself, couldn't help it. There were no secrets, no masks that worked, no escape from what you were. What I was was a failure who had to act like he wasn't. Only then would the narcs not get me.

So now I had something to tell Hilton. I wrote on the paper, between the blue lines: "I am so sorry, man. Don't flip. I know you will make it."

I stared at the words. The handwriting was childishly neat, not mine at all. But it was. I signed it, put it in the envelope, finished addressing it, licked the stamps and stuck them on. I stood up. I was sweating. I was in a great hurry.

"Where are you going?" said Kay.

"I have to go. I have to get this to Hilton."

"Oh God. I'll go with you."

As we walked out, me holding the letter goofily in both hands, I thought everyone was watching me, seeing me as I had just seen them. Then I realized they couldn't, they would just think I was crazy. Maybe I was. Maybe

I had cracked and didn't know it. Scott Fitzgerald said that when you cracked you didn't really know it. The first thing is the crack, but it seems like just another bad attack, tough to handle, but you handled it, just like you always did. And then one morning you wake up knowing that what you thought was just temporarily missing will never come back.

I remember, now, mailing the letter at the corner, and Kay's reproaching me, as we walked to her place, for any number of things: for turning on, for being determined to demean myself, for "continually postulating a rejection" of her. Everything she said, it seemed, was true. I couldn't reasonably disagree. Except that later, as I lay in her soft, back-breaking bed, my mind, like a relentless newsreel, ground out this scene, against which even Kay could have no defense: I was shouting, raging, sobbing, and Betty was trying to be hard and unswayed. "Let's call it quits," she said. I held her, kissed her. "We'll have to remember this for a long time," I said. She started to cry then too.

Kay was asleep. I leaned over her to turn on the radio. She kept sleeping. Asleep she did not seem so oppressive, and I had softened thoughts toward her. Not tender, but at least tolerant. I felt like a heel. I had known all the time I would not be able to resist those great breasts, the soft tyranny of her assurance-craving desire. Just as I had known I would not be able to kid myself for long. Having a movie camera for a brain knocks hell out of your virility. Well, she said, she didn't require anything. I touched her, she told me, she felt I needed somebody, and all in the world she wanted was to help. I hadn't believed that for a minute, but I believed she believed it, which made it worse. Nevertheless, there I was, in bed with a militant radical. Maybe someday I would be militant myself, if I ever got clear on what was going on.

The jazz station came on with a Charlie Parker side. Hilton and I had known it well. It was called "Hot House" but was really a variation of "What Is This Thing Called Love." In this case love was a mish-mash of machine-gun notes that only Bird could put together right. *Poor Bird,* I thought. *Poor Hilton, busted. Poor me, in bed with a radical chick who kept offering herself to me as if I had something to give.* And I was on a reality kick! Reality was here in bed with me, and it smelled and felt and tasted just like me. I couldn't wait till morning. I put my clothes on and got out of there.

LESTER AND BILLIE JEAN

When I was fifteen, in my first year of high school, I had this great crush on Billie Jean Bascomb. I'd never had a girl friend, or even a friend who was a girl, never had the nerve to ask anyone for a date, never could even figure out how to say it. I wanted to ask Billie Jean to a movie or a dance, but when I tried to imagine asking her, the sentence would break up in pieces.

Finally, the week after Thanksgiving, after endless rehearsal on the exact words, I finally screwed up the nerve to call her. After four rings, giddy with relief that no one was home, I was about to hang up when I heard her voice.

"Billie Jean?" I stammered.

"Yes?" Bright, expectant, as if she had been waiting for me, just me, to call.

I blurted out my "would you like" speech about the Christmas dance three weeks from then.

"But won't you be playing in the band?"

"Actually, they've hired a professional band, Dick Barrett."

"Oh, they're good. Well, I guess, sure, I'd love to. Will you be at the dance tomorrow?"

I hadn't asked her to the dance the next night because, besides being in the band, I had absorbed the idea somewhere, probably in that Dr. Wiggam psychology column my mother was always cutting out of the newspaper, that to be polite you had to give girls a lot of notice.

"Yeah, I'll be playing with the great Count Grootin, ha ha."

"Super, I'll see you then."

So I actually had a date with cute little Billie Jean. She was flat-chested, but big tits scared me silly, and I loved her turned-up nose and the way she stood in the hall with saddle-shoed feet together, laughing and chattering and hugging her books.

Once Sammy Crofts and I rode our bikes in the rain down to her house in San Marino, where all the bankers lived. Sammy, who played drums in Count Grootin's band, lived in an old four-unit apartment house near me with his divorced mother and two sisters. He was tall and skinny with red hair, a faceful of pimples, and a big knotty adam's apple, but he had a crazy nerve with girls.

We circled around in the street for awhile, Sammy saying come on, let's go see her, girls are just like us, they like attention. I didn't believe girls were just like us, so Sammy went to the front door while I sat on my bike in the street, rain falling on my bare head and streaming down my yellow slicker. Somebody opened the door, and Sammy waved me to come on.

Billie Jean's mother herded us off the living room rug and into the kitchen, where Billie Jean had a bunch of beads spread out on the table, making a necklace. Sammy sat down and told her how pretty the beads were, how his sisters were always making necklaces and stuff, and where did she learn to do that? I just stood there, shuffling and grinning and worrying about catching the flu. A puddle was forming on the linoleum at my feet. After about ten minutes her mother said Billie Jean had to go to her dance class. Sammy tuned in on that right now: "I bet you're a super dancer." She laughed, oh no, not really.

As we rode home Sammy told me again about girls, how you had to flatter them, let them know how great you thought they were. I didn't understand. If a girl caught me staring at her, I'd turn away and pretend I wasn't. I'd feel she'd caught me doing something gross and shameful. And most of the time she had, because my eyes were gobbling up her tits.

All that time when I didn't call her, I was practicing my clarinet or my new tenor saxophone and imagining her admiring how great I played. I'd been studying clarinet for three years, but the saxophone for less than a year. I'd taken it up after my teacher, Mr. Adams, played some Lester Young-Count Basie records for me and got me trying to play jazz. Like everyone else, I knew all about Benny Goodman and Glen Miller, but I had also heard a lot of the black bands--Duke Ellington, Erskine Hawkins, Jimmie Lunceford, bands like that. And when Mr. Adams first played me "I Want a Little Girl," with Lester Young on clarinet, I just wanted to cry, it sounded so sweet, so sad.

It took me all summer to learn that solo off the record. The notes weren't that hard, but Mr. Adams wouldn't even let me play it until I could sing it just right, not just the notes but the timing, the feel. Meanwhile he was playing me more Lester Young with Basie, all on tenor, and as soon as I heard that--"Lady Be Good," "Jumpin' at the Woodside," "Every Tub"--I was crazy to play tenor. Mr. Adams found a Conn that belonged to some guy who got drafted and had hardly played it, and my parents bought it for me for 60 bucks.

When school started in the fall, one of my classes was algebra, with Mr. Grootin. He played bass fiddle and was famous as the teacher who organized bands for dances. Everyone who wanted to be in his band was in the class, including me, Sammy, a fat kid named Lennie Epatkin who played trumpet, and plain Jane Hardaway with her wounded donkey laugh. For auditions Mr. Grootin had each of us play something we knew, alone, and then he put a band part in front of us to see if we could read.

My solo piece was, of course, "I Want a Little Girl." I had decided to play clarinet for the audition because I didn't feel comfortable on tenor yet. I played Lester's intro and the melody first, and that settled me down. Then I played Lester's solo. There's a part where it jumps down an octave, comes back up on the E arpeggio, and then plays an A triad into D, and I got a little flustered and almost fluffed a couple notes. But it wasn't too bad.

"Ah," said the Count. Mr. Grootin liked to call himself Count, after Basie. "Very nice. A budding Benny Goodman."

"That was Lester Young," I said, embarrassed. "I like him better."

Raised eyebrows from the other kids, a guffaw from Lennie, who'd never heard of Lester but thought nobody could possibly be better than Benny Goodman. Lennie idolized Goodman's trumpet player, Harry James. James was flashy, no doubt about it. But I liked Benny Carter's trumpet better, and he was really an alto sax player.

"I didn't know," said Count, "that Lester Young had recorded on clarinet."

27

"On Commodore," I said. "The Kansas City Six.".

He wanted to hear me play tenor, so we read through "Tuxedo Junction," an easy tune. That's when I became a member of the band, Count Grootin and His Hot Seven Minus Two. The Count had to get his math in there. Besides me there was poor Jane on piano--she sounded awful corny but she could read--the Count on bass, Sammy on drums, and Mr. Flash-Ass Lennie on trumpet.

Before Thanksgiving we had only played for a couple of noon dances, nothing at night. So this night, the day after I got the date with Billie Jean, was our night-time debut. We had been rehearsing things like "Johnson's Rag," "Begin the Beguine," and of course "In the Mood." On a couple of blues, like "Woodchopper's Ball," I would improvise my tenor solo. I was still shaky on making what was in my head come out right on the horn, so I mostly just played what was written. Because of me, the Count had added "I Want a Little Girl" to our book, with me on clarinet. We did it just the way it was on the record: Lester's four-bar introduction, trumpet on the written melody, then me with Lester's solo, followed by the trumpet lead on the bridge and the last eight bars.

My parents were at a church fund-raiser, and Sammy's mother was out on a date, so Sammy's sister Carmen had to drive us to the dance. Carmen was going with this leather-jacketed motorcycle guy and was pissed off that she had to break up her evening driving us.

Sammy was in a funny mood. He kept aiming out the window with his finger and going "Pow!" Then he would let out a big guffaw. I was in a state myself, somewhere between ecstasy and terror, thinking about Billie Jean.

We pulled up at the gym where the dance was and started stacking Sammy's snare and cymbals and bass drum and toms and my two horns on the sidewalk. The second we finished, Carmen, grimacing and jamming a half-smoked cigarette in the ashtray, actually burned rubber as she took off. While I was staring at the tail end of their oil-burning Ford, Sammy grabbed my arm.

"Look what I got." He reached in his stick bag and pulled out a pearl-handled revolver. "Is that pretty or what?"

"Where'd you get it? What's it for?" I had never seen one except in the movies. It looked huge.

He was spinning the chamber, showing me the six bullets.

"It's a beauty, huh? I borrowed it off Jeff, Carmen's boy friend. And I got these."

He pulled out a Sir Walter Raleigh tobacco tin and an envelope full of red capsules.

"I'm in business, man."

"Selling pipe tobacco? What are the red things?"

"Uppers, man. Benzedrine. And this ain't tobacco."

Sammy had already been hauled into the vice-principal's office for smoking and drinking beer between classes. Now here he was with this stuff.

A car pulled up alongside us. Sammy, his back turned, crammed everything back in his stick case. The Count got out the driver's side and came around to pull his bass out of the back seat.

"Nice to see you two here bright and early. Need help?" We shook our heads, and he went up the steps with the bass.

I had been trying to calm myself about Billie Jean and our Christmas date and playing "I Want a Little Girl" for her. But now Sammy and his gun and his dope had caused things to jangle, like the band in charge of mood music had suddenly started playing in three keys at once.

"Why do you have the gun? Why is it loaded?"

"Self defense, man. You can't deal without being able to protect yourself. And what's the good of having a gun if you have to run around looking for bullets when the time comes to shoot?"

"Who you looking to shoot?"

"How do I know? I'm selling merchandise that certain individuals might want to grab from me. Like O'Malley, maybe, or Frickert." Stoop-shouldered, evil-eyed Billy O'Malley was our class bad boy. Frickert was his big, raw-boned sidekick.

Sammy was holding out a hand-rolled cigarette, twisted at one end. At that time I'd never seen a joint. "What is it?"

"Gage, man. Weed. Reefer. Marijuana. And if you start to nod out, we've got the uppers."

I could see he loved saying those words. I had to guess what "nod out" meant.

I was curious, but I had never done stuff like that, not even beer. One time my daddy gave me a taste of beer and I thought it was awful. "I don't want any."

Sammy shrugged. "The store's still open. But I need for you to take this stuff and hide it for me. Old Stevens would never suspect you of anything." Stevens was the vice principal, who would chaperone the dance.

"You're crazy," I said. But I opened my tenor case and stuck the stuff in. The gun, cold and heavy in my hand, filled up the compartment. There was hardly room for my mouthpiece and reeds. I wanted Sammy to take out the bullets, but I wanted even more to get it out of sight. I covered it with my cleaning rag and shut the case.

31

We hauled our stuff up into the girls' gym. The dance was in the girls' gym because there was an upright piano that the girls' gym teacher used. For what I didn't know. There was no piano in the boys' gym. We set up by the piano, in the far corner. Jane arrived and started practicing her parts in her clunky style. By the time Flash-Ass Lennie got there to thrill the night air with his "Sleepy Lagoon" vibrato, the metal folding chairs along the walls were filling up, girls on one side and boys on the other. I didn't see Billie Jean. When we were ready to start, Sammy wasn't behind his set. Then he came zooting across the floor, grinning and snapping his fingers, head bobbing on his long Adam's-apple neck.

"Sorry. Call of nature," he said cheerily, settling down on his stool and rapping off a roll and cymbal crash.

We started off with "Moonlight Serenade," the Glen Miller theme song. A combo like ours has a hard time sounding like the whole Glen Miller sax section, but nobody cared. I had the lead on clarinet. Flash-Ass Lennie had a harmony part but he kept playing over me. I had to blow louder, trying to keep him from taking over. He flustered me, but I made the high notes and the little accelerando at the end. People clapped. I looked for Billie Jean but still didn't see her. We went through our play-list: "Johnson's Rag," where I took a lame tenor solo in Eb, a hard key for me; "How Come You Do Me Like You Do Do Do," in A, another of my least favorite keys; "Star Dust," in which Lennie delivered his sob-sister

Harry James vibrato and several clams; and "Begin the Beguine," which featured me as Artie Shaw but which has a glissando at the end which I had to fake, just playing regular notes, because I hadn't learned to gliss. I didn't sound like Artie Shaw, and that, plus my boring tenor solos, made me feel like a jerk, a phony.

When break time came, I still hadn't seen Billie Jean. I was relieved she hadn't heard the mediocre stuff I played. But mostly I was getting a sinking feeling. Maybe she wasn't even coming. She didn't want to see me, I'd been kidding myself that she liked me. I made my way across the floor to the porch outside. I looked back, and there she was, standing with her back to me, talking to a guy and a couple of girls. But instead of going to her, I panicked and ran down the stairs to the locker room. I was pacing around and around when this guy Harlan came down and said Billie Jean wanted to see me. He was one of those San Marino guys who got a haircut every two weeks and always wore cashmere sweaters with the sleeves pulled up to just below the elbow. My heart jumped. She actually asked for me! I went up the stairs feeling like I was in a fun house with crazy mirrors, wondering what stupid ugly version of me would come next, scared out of my wits.

Billie Jean was talking to her buddies, Barbara Ludmiller and Evie Curtis. I went up to her, my heart knocking in my throat.

"Oh Collis!" she said. "I've been looking for you."

"I thought you weren't here yet," I lied.

"We were late." The record that people were dancing to was Flash-Ass's favorite, "Sleepy Lagoon" by Harry James.

"I love Harry James, don't you?" said Billie Jean.

"You wanta dance?" I stammered.

I didn't know how to dance, I just kind of rocked back and forth, holding her. I was getting a hard-on.

"Collis," she started in, pulling away. "I've been thinking. It was awfully nice of you to ask me to the Christmas dance, so early and all. That was very considerate, really. The only thing is, my parents are talking about taking a trip before Christmas, and if we do, then I won't be able to go with you, and I would hate to--I mean, I won't know for a week or so and I don't think I should leave you wondering if I'm going to go with you or not, so maybe we should not commit ourselves now, and if I can't go then you would have time to ask someone else, and if you did, you know, that would be all right with me, because there would still be time, if my parents didn't take a trip after all, there would still be time for someone else to ask me, and we'd see each other at the dance, and, I know it's a lot to ask, and you were very sweet to ask me so early, but really, would you mind?"

Something in me wanted to feel the hammer hit me dead-on, between the eyes.

"Would I mind what?"

Her smile started turning into something less diplomatic.

"You know," she said reproachfully. Suddenly she stuck out her chin and leaned forward. "If we broke our date. I want to go with Harlan."

Behind her I got a blurred image of Barbara and Evie and cashmere Harlan, watching and waiting. I stumbled blindly toward the door, bouncing off dancing couples like a pin ball. I was trying to keep from falling down the steps to the street when Sammy grabbed me by the shoulder.

"Wait up, man! I saw you talking to Billie Jean. What happened?"

"She broke it off. She wants to go with Harlan."

"Rich fucking San Marino bastards." He put his arm on my shoulder, then looked around, to see if anyone was watching.

"Collis, my man, it's time for you to discover the joys of chemistry. Take a puff of this."

He held out the lighted joint in his hand. I'd never smoked even regular cigarettes. I tried it once, inhaling, and it made me sick.

"How do you do it?"

Sammy led me up the street, away from the lights.

"You just draw the smoke in your mouth, and then you let it go down your throat real slow and sort of swallow it, and then hold your breath as long as you can. The longer the smoke stays in, the more you get."

I took a long, slow drag.

"Now suck in, real slow or it'll burn your throat. Take it easy. Hold it there, don't breathe out."

I held it in as long as I could. I wanted to be out of my mind.

"Take another."

I did.

"Nothing's happening," I said, disappointed.

"Patience," said Sammy. "Take some more. We got to finish this before we go back."

We smoked it down to where it burned our fingers. Sammy put the butt in a little Bayer aspirin tin.

As we walked back to the gym, a full moon was coming up over the trees down the street. As I watched, it got bigger, lighting up the storm clouds that had gathered. Suddenly I realized I had been looking at the moon forever, standing and staring with my mouth open. I turned around, looking away from the moon. The clouds in that direction were dark, scary. I turned back, drinking the brightness. Then, looking down, I saw the writing in the dirt along the sidewalk, some kind of twisty Sanscrit. I stooped down, trying to decipher it, when I realized they were tree roots that had cracked the surface of the ground around the trees.

Seeing me stooped over, reading the tree roots, Sammy giggled.

"Something happening now?"

"Oh yeah," I said.

Sammy put a red capsule in my hand. "Better take this in case you've had too much."

As we climbed the steps, Sammy waved to Mr. Stevens standing at his observation post on the porch. Mr. Stevens nodded, following us with gimlet eyes as we turned the corner to the water fountain inside, where we washed our bennies down. As we passed into the gym, Stevems still had his eyes on us, making sure we didn't sneak down to the locker room to jack off.

"Easy does it," said Sammy. I thought I must look like a humpback idiot, but nobody seemed to notice. I didn't even look for Billie Jean. I could see her in my mind, sticking her chin out, saying, "I want to go with Harlan."

The Count was waiting for us, ready to start. Our first tune was "Tuxedo Junction," with me on tenor. In that song the same phrase gets repeated over and over. I got locked into it, and when the little triplet figures came in the bridge, I wasn't ready for them. The first rule in reading music is look ahead, never be surprised. And here I was surprised by the slowest and easiest tune in our book. The reed was squeaking on me, I was playing clams I never played before. I looked out and saw Billie Jean and Harlan, his arm around her waist, one of her hands patting him playfully on the chest. Naughty, naughty. I looked at the play list. Coming up was "I Want a Little Girl." I shook my head no, no. The Count gave me a little calm-down wave and pointed commandingly to my clarinet. I picked it up, feeling like I was being blindfolded for the firing squad.

The Count gave the beat, and I surprised myself by doing the intro perfectly. Then Lennie took the lead, and I started to hate what I was hearing. First of all, he was supposed to use his mute, but he forgot, giving it his phony vibrato full bore, and then he fell in with Jane's ricky-ticky phrasing, and the whole thing went wrong. I could feel the dope sending me off into a time-warp.

I tried to hear Buck Clayton and Freddie Green in my head, like on the record. When I started Lester's solo, I was able to straighten it out a little. But Jane's phrasing was so corny, so un-Basie, that four bars into the chorus, where the big jumps come, I lost Lester's flow and grabbed at some notes of my own. The dope told me they were good notes, oh everything was groovy, real original, you're blazing new trails, but there was that other voice saying I was making a mess of Lester's beautiful solo, and in front of Billie Jean. In the last four bars I managed to get back to Lester, but by that time I wanted to crawl behind the piano and disappear.

When it was over I looked out on the floor. Billie Jean had said something funny. Harlan was doubled over laughing. At me, of course. I dived down into a boiling pool of humiliation. While I was there, the Count's count-off of the next tune went right by me.

"Won't you join us, Collis?" said the Count. "'Ain't She Sweet,' okay?"

That made me giggle and almost cry at the same time. Then we were playing the tune when suddenly I felt myself charging through it like a wild horse through butter. Lennie stopped playing, and I saw the Count giving me this desperate look and shaking his head. I realized the benzedrine had just kicked in and I'd been rushing something awful. It was a struggle to keep in the time for the last two tunes.

We started packing up. My fingers were shaking.

"You okay?" said the Count. "You don't look so good."

"I'm sorry," I said.

"Don't worry about it. Nobody knows the difference."

Yeah, I thought to myself, *they do. They know what makes them feel good and what doesn't.* I bungled. I can't take it back. The bad notes, the time, they all happened, they're out there, you can't hear them anymore but they're there in the air. Air to air, dust to dust. I should be dust. Those notes made of my air had merged with the air of Billie Jean's "I want to go with Harlan" and become the poison air I breathed. How did it happen that two of the worst things I could imagine had just perpetrated themselves, and I was still alive, not dust? Or if it was just the memory that was doing this to me, kill the memory, kill me. I should be dead.

I ran the chamois through my clarinet and put it in its case. I opened my tenor case. Under the cleaning rag was Sammy's stuff. I couldn't give anything back to him now. I cleaned the neck and mouthpiece, put the reed in its cardboard holder, covered everything again with the rag. Sammy broke down his set. We hauled our gear out to the curb just as Carmen screeched to a stop at the curb. "Hurry up," she yelled. "I ain't got all night."

We loaded our gear and got in, barely getting the door closed before Carmen was burning rubber again taking off. Clouds were inching over the big fat moon.

"So she dumped you," said Sammy. "So you messed up the time. So what? Next time, right? Plenty of gigs, plenty of fish in the sea. Don't worry about the stuff in your case. I don't want my mom finding it. I'll call you tomorrow."

When they let me off at my house, my parents were already in bed. They'd left the hall light on for me. I turned it out and started upstairs. I could feel myself coming down, way down, off the benny. At the turn in the stairs, through the little window, I watched the clouds moving over the moon, the moon going slowly out, the dark spilling down. *It always goes out,* I thought. *Never there when you need it. A fake, doesn't even have its own light. Just a cold dead hunk of rock pretending to be this great romantic thing.*

I sat on my bed in the dark, my tenor case beside me. The moon was out. I was out. I opened the tenor case and ran my hand over the keys. *It's the dope,* I thought, *it's the benzedrine bottoming out, taking me with it. I ought to stop it, I thought, but I don't even want to, I'm falling in love with it.* I took out Sammy's gun. It was heavy. I held it in my lap, staring at it.

Look at that, I thought. *There it is, the answer to all your problems. No more Billie Jean, no more bad time, no more pathetic imitations of Lester Young. One simple gesture and you're all drained out, the tub is empty.* My tub. "Every Tub." Is that what that song title meant? What would it be like? I opened my mouth, like for the doctor, to say "Ah." I stuck the barrel in, closed my teeth and lips around it. Hard, cold. My right index finger was crooked around the trigger. I heard Billie Jean saying, "I want to go with Harlan." I heard myself butchering Lester's solo. It wasn't that hard, Mr. Adams said, and I knew that was true. But I screwed it up. I didn't expect to screw it up, I thought I had it. What happened? *Billie Jean,* said a voice, *Billie Jean happened. You thought you had her too. You needed her, and she turned on you. She wasn't what you thought.* There was a long silence. *But,* said the voice, after what seemed like forever, *Lester is still Lester.*

I took the gun out of my mouth and passed out. The next day, Saturday, I got up at noon and practiced for six hours straight. Scales, scales in thirds, triads and arpeggios, in every major and minor key, chromatics, diminished and augmented scales and chords. From that day I became a practicing demon. It took me four years, but I learned those Lester Young solos Mr. Adams had played for me and a whole bunch of others, including the ones he just made, "Just You, Just Me" and "Sometimes I'm Happy." So beautiful.

THE SKINHEAD GIG

When Artie called, I was in the middle of one of my wandering dreams. This guy I could hardly understand had appeared to guide me. He talked in a weird, mumbling way, took me to a house where Mafia types glided by, giving me the once-over with nasty little smirks on their faces.

"We got a gig tonight," said Artie.

"Short notice, isn't it?"

"It's a fraternity, sort of. A rock band canceled out on them. Must've got a better gig."

"If they wanted a rock band, how come they got us?"

"I know this guy whose cousin runs with them. They were a little desperate."

Safford Chamberlain

"We don't know any rock tunes."

"We know blues. We know 'Watermelon Man.' George can play with a big back beat."

"I can hear it. 'Green Dolphin Street' with a rock back beat. Who's playing guitar?"

"You. You're the guitar."

I play tenor saxophone. Don't call it a sax, it's a saxophone. My all-time hero is The Prez, Lester Young. Of course I listened to rock when I was a kid, in junior high school, but when my teacher played Lester's "Lady Be Good" for me, that was it. Recorded in 1936, I couldn't believe it. I'm no Prez, nobody is, but over the years, I learned every note in that solo, and a bunch of others--"Broadway," "Tickletoe," "Song of the Islands"-- you name it, I can play it. The last thing I want to sound like is a heavy metal guitarist.

"Artie, I don't have a good feeling about this gig. What fraternity is it?"

"It's not exactly a fraternity. It's sort of a social club, in a private home."

"Where?"

"Fontana."

Fontana is fifty miles east of L.A., in the part of the San Gabriel Valley that in another forty miles evaporates into the Mojave desert. Gusty winds are always blowing in Fontana. There used to be a Kaiser steel mill there. Now I read about racist skinheads stashing guns and beating up on people. Artie is black, and our bass player, Rueben, is Latino and East Indian. Me, I'm Jewish, or at least my parents are.

"No. No deal. Forget it."

"Fifty bucks. Fifty apiece."

"We have to drive a hundred miles, plus that place is a nest of what my pinko parents call fascist swine. Skinheads, you know? The guys that beat that Ethiopian student to death at a bus stop in Portland? It's not worth it."

"Not worth it?" says Artie. "Come on, man, we get to play, we get to make our music and get paid for it. It'll be so fucking beautiful the fascist swine will get down on their knees and lick our boots. Besides, there won't be any fascist swine, it's just a social club."

I could see Artie wanted this. We hadn't had all that many paying gigs lately. Two weddings, to be precise, the last one two months ago.

"If we wear boots. Give me a couple hours."

By the time I got to Artie's--he pretty much lives in his parents' garage, which he's fixed up as a studio--George and Reuben were already there, setting up. We ran over "Watermelon Man" and "You Are the Sunshine of My Life" and a couple of blues in different keys with heavy back beats.

"Okay, that's the first set," I said. "Then what do we do?"

Artie handed us a list of tunes.

"'I'm Getting Sentimental Over You?'" I read. 'Body and Soul?' What happened to that great rock classic 'Hey Baby, Ooo, Oww, Give It to Me, Fuck My Brains Out?'"

Artie shrugged. "We got to educate these people."

"Sure," I said. "I just hope they don't want to educate us."

The gig was for eight o'clock. We loaded Artie's twelve-year-old Chevy van and left a lttle after six, plenty of time, under normal circumstances. Unfortunately they weren't normal. At West Covina, coming up the big hill before Pomona, we hit a massive traffic jam. Nothing was moving. We were between off-ramps and couldn't even get off the freeway. Artie turned on the radio, and we learned that a semi had jack-knifed and caused a multi-car pile-up. People had been killed. We couldn't do a thing but sit there.

"We're going to be late," I said.

"Dear me, the skinheads will be mad," said Artie.

"You didn't tell me this was a skinhead party," said George. George has a great time-feel, but he's a worrier.

"He's just kidding," I said. "It's just a social club."

"No, really," said Artie. "Fontana is a nest of fascist swine. Everybody there belongs to the White Ayran Resistance. They dine on niggers, kykes, and greasers. But you'll be okay, George."

"Screw you," said George. It was just what made his time-feel so great. When things got serious, he forgot to worry, or hurry.

"As long as we're professional," he said, in his dead-serious tone. George was a stickler for being professional.

"We'll all be ooo-kay," said Reuben the peacemaker. Whenever Rueben says something like that, something in you says, "Wow! Loving-kindness rules the world!"

"Damn right we will," said Artie.

Finally the traffic started to move. The semi was still on its side across three lanes. Up ahead we could see a tow truck moving off with a crumpled car hulk. Three or four cop cars were lined up on the shoulder, red, yellow, and blue lights flashing. The roadway was littered with glass. A cop kicked a hubcap off to the side. I looked for bodies in white sheets but didn't see any.

We were an hour late in Fontana. There was a lot of tension in the air as they let us in.

"Sorry we're late," said Artie. "There was a pile-up on the freeway."

Most of them didn't look like skinheads. They looked like bowlers and weekend tag fooball players and girls who just wanta have fun. Some of them even wore ties.

"Must have been some pile-up," one guy said. I checked him out. He looked something like a skinhead. His crew-cut was out of Marine boot camp, his broad plug-ugly face and broken nose straight out of Rams' free-agent tryouts.

Artie stared at him.

"It was."

"Was anybody hurt?" It was the girl next to Plug-Ugly, in a red satin dress, the hem several inches above the knee. She had great legs, nice tits with cleavage showing.

"As a matter of fact, yeah," said Artie. "A semi jack-knifed. People died. We heard it on the radio."

"How awful," said the girl in red.

"They're an hour late," grumbled her boy friend. "That's what's awful."

"Horace is the sensitive type," said the girl, making a face, looking at Plug-Ugly, then Artie. "You guys are lucky you weren't in the pile-up. We're glad you made it."

"Yeah," said Artie. "Us too."

But Plug-Ugly wasn't finished.

"If we just quit all this sensitive bullshit," said Horace, glaring at the girl, "maybe they'll play some music for us. If they know how. You think you can do that?"

"Look," said Artie, "we're sorry we're late. It wasn't our fault. It will take us a few minutes to set up. Where's an outlet?"

A tall, skinny Latino guy with long black hair stepped up.

"I'm Al, Manuel's cousin." He had a nice quiet smile, like Reuben.

"You're the one who called us?"

"Yeah." He gave a little apologetic shrug. "I like straight-ahead, you know? There's an outlet over here by the couch."

It was nice to know we had one fan. George set up his drums, Artie plugged in his Yamaha and Reuben his bass, and we were ready to go.

We started with Bird's "Now's the Time." It's basically the old "Hucklebuck," one of the early rock 'n' roll hits, very danceable. It's a blues, of course. When it came around for me to solo I felt good, in spite of the wreck on the freeway, in spite of Plug-Ugly Horace and all the hassle. I knew what I played wasn't what they were programmed to hear, but the time felt so right I didn't care. I had some tension of my own to let off.

When I stopped my solo, there was no applause, but they were dancing, and I figured that was about the same as applause for a non-jazz audience. The girl in red was twirling around jitterbug style, showing off a lot of leg and glimpses of red satin ass. Her partner wasn't Plug-Ugly but Al, Manuel's quiet-smiling but, as I could see, slick-moving cousin.

Artie didn't do much his first chorus, just some close-voiced chords spaced out Basie-style, trying to get a feel, listening to George and Reuben. In the second chorus he sketched out a line, still with a lot of space, and then he began to fill it in. It's beautiful, the way Artie builds a solo. As I listened I felt myself coming back from wherever I had been since we passed the accident.

We got a nice hand when we finished, so Artie decided to go with another of Bird's blues, a Latin piece in the same key but a brighter tempo, called "Barbadoes." After that we eased into "Watermelon Man." Things seemed to have settled into a groove when Plug-Ugly showed up again.

He stood there in front of us, swaying a little, his shirttail hanging out over his beer belly and a 16-ounce can of Colt 45 in his hand.

"You guys know any real music? Something a white man can dance to?"

Artie stared at him. I knew what was going through his head, and so did Plug-Ugly. But Artie cooled it.

"'In the Mood,'" he said to us, winking. It was Artie's idea of a joke, the whitest music he could think of short of Lawrence Welk. We started it, Glen Miller style, me doing the traditional tenor and alto exchange, pretending to be both Tex Beneke and whoever Miller's alto player was.

In the middle of my duet with myself it started to rain. I opened my eyes. Plug-Ugly was spraying me with his beer can, whether intentionally or accidentally I couldn't tell. My face was dripping. So was my horn.

I put my horn down in its stand. Plug-Ugly was standing there belly out, laughing like a maniac. I thought about kicking him in the nuts and smashing my fist in his face. It would have been easy, he was such a drunken klutz. Maybe if he had called me jewboy I would have. But I just stared at him.

"I need a kleenex," I said.

The girl in red reached into her cleavage and came out with a couple of kleenexes, waving them like a white flag.

When I took them I could feel they were damp and sweaty. I didn't want her sweat all over my horn. Sweat corrodes brass, and my horn doesn't have any lacquer. The last time I had a horn relacquered, it ruined the sound.

"I need dry ones," I said.

She blushed. "I've got some in my purse."

She went to where she had stashed her purse and rushed over to give me some dry ones. I wiped off my face. Then I got down on one knee and started wiping off my horn.

Behind me I could hear people trying to cool off Plug-Ugly.

"Fuck it!" he was yelling. "These guys can't play shit. Who hired this spook and his mongrel band anyway?"

Behind the words he actually sounded a little ashamed of himself, like he was pretending to be hotter than he was. I wondered where he got "mongrel."

"I did," said Al, Manuel's cousin, stepping forward.

"You got a taste for shit," said Plug-Ugly. "And stay away from my girl friend."

"But I have a taste for your girl friend," said Al. "I think she's a real sweet lady. Do you call that a taste for shit?"

Al was cool, maybe too cool.

"Stop it!" shouted the girl in red, stepping between them, flailing at Plug-Ugly, pounding on his chest. "Damn you, Horace! We were just dancing, there's nothing going on! Why do you have to act like this?"

With the help of others, she managed to herd Plug-Ugly into the kitchen.

I looked at Artie. He looked back, rolled his eyes, and started an intro to "There Is No Greater Love." Yeah, I thought, there is no greater love than to love that cretin. Yet, a couple of tunes later, when we were playing "Sweet Lorraine," a pretty ballad I've always liked, there they were, Plug-Ugly and the girl in red, slow-dancing cheek to cheek, belly to belly. He was a little wobbly, but she held him steady.

It was time for a break. I found a beer in the kitchen and wandered out into the front yard with Artie and the guys.

"Some gig," said George. He turned to me. "You were cool, man. Real professional. And Artie...."

He was going to go on, but Artie gave him a look. I turned around, and there was the girl in red.

"Hi there," said Artie.

"I want to apologize," she said. "For Horace."

"Why?" said George. "Like, what did he do?"

That broke the ice a little. She was on the verge of tears.

"He's not really like that. He's confused. He thinks people are against him."

"Because he's white, perhaps?" said Artie sarcastically.

"No, no, it's not really a race thing. He might think that's it, but it's not. He thinks he's ugly, that people see him as stupid and ugly, a dumb jock. He hates his broken nose, but he can't afford to get it fixed. He thinks I don't love him, but I do."

"Pardon me for asking," I said, "but what, exactly...?"

"Why, you mean? Aw, Christ, I don't...." She slapped both hands over her mouth and started to cry. "There I go again, taking the name of the Lord in vain! I don't know, I just do. He's not like you saw him. He can be warm, and, and protective. I don't know why, I just do."

"Well," said Artie, "he was a little out of control there. Let's hope his insecurities don't lead him any further down the primrose path of racist indiscretion."

That, with the edge in Artie's voice, sounded a little harsh to me. Maybe not to her. She didn't seem the type to pick up on Artie's kind of irony.

"Maybe you can talk to him," I said.

"I will," she said. She wiped her eyes with a kleenex from her cleavage stash and blew her nose. "I definitely will. I think he should apologize. I will tell him that."

She gave us a determined smile, still blowing her nose, and backed away toward the house.

"Easy does it," said Artie softly, watching her go.

The next set went pretty well. We started with our Stevie Wonder tune, 'You Are the Sunshine of My Life." It's actually a decent tune to blow on. What's the difference if it's Jerome Kern or Stevie Wonder if you can blow on it?

They liked it, as Artie figured they would. So now we started our educational program: "Body and Soul," "I'm Getting Sentimental Over You," "Lady Be Good." On "Lady" we don't begin with Gershwin's melody but start right in with Prez's incredible solo, Artie and I playing it in unison before I start the blowing.

Plug-Ugly and the girl in red were dancing right in front of us. On "Body and Soul" they just held each other and swayed. On "Sentimental" he looked clumsy, but she kept him going, faking his lead, spinning around, coming back in his arms. She had him thinking he was pretty good.

At the end of "Sentimental" she turned him toward us, holding his hand, beaming.

"Horace wants to say something."

From the look he gave her, Horace was not crazy about this. But he was trying to be a good boy.

"Yeah," he said. "Well, I'm sorry."

They exchanged looks.

"For, like, spraying you. And saying you couldn't play."

Another eye exchange.

"What?" he said. "You wanted me to apologize, I apologized. What now?"

"The rest of it," she said. "What we talked about."

"Aw, get off me, leave me alone." He hitched his shoulders up and jerked his head from side to side, as if she were actually riding him.

"You promised, Horace."

"I did it. I apologized."

"You called him a spook. You talked about music a white man can dance to."

That was too much for him.

"So I'm white and he's black," he snarled, "and I said so. I got to apologize for that? We're paying them, they're supposed to be playing for us. We're white, and they're giving us this nigger music that twists your ears, jazz or whatever it is. All I want is music for us, for white people!"

Artie stepped around in front of his keyboard.

"I've had about enough of this racist diatribe," he said. "I think I'll kick your ugly honky ass."

That pulled Horace's trigger. He drew back his right arm, but before he could throw the punch the girl in red grabbed his wrist. With about a hundred and twenty pounds hanging on his arm, he got twisted backwards and nearly fell over. She lost her grip, and when he came back up he swung a backhand that knocked her halfway across the room. As he straightened up, Al, Manuel's cousin, launched a beautiful overhand right that caught him precisely on the point of his chin. He landed in the girl's lap, out cold between her legs, his head on her belly, she with blood trickling from the corner of her mouth and an upper lip that was already getting fat.

"Play something," said Al, rubbing his right fist with his other hand.

Some people were pulling the girl in red to her feet. Others were dragging Horace into the kitchen.

I looked at Artie. He was in another world, watching Horace's feet disappear through the kitchen doorway. We hadn't played "Lady Be Good" yet. I looked at Reuben and George.

"Bar and a half," I said, and started counting into the pickup. Somewhere near the middle of Prez's first chorus Artie joined us. As we finished our unison on Prez's solo, Artie gave me a look and I let him take it. At first what he was playing seemed to come right out of Prez's head, but then Artie started turning in some directions Prez never thought to go. Prez was all swinging sweetness and light. It never occurred to him to put in what drove him crazy, at least not till after he was drafted and thrown in the stockade for smoking pot, and even then his playing was sad, not angry.

I didn't really want to follow what Artie was doing, but I saw from his expression that if I chickened out I would never hear the end of it, so I started in. Sometimes you don't have a clue, you don't even know what note you're starting on, but something's been switched on without your knowing, and it comes. It's a kind of what-have-I-got-to-lose, this-is-where-I'm-at feeling. You just groove down in the time and play from someplace inside, not worrying about matching whatever great stuff went before, like Artie's solo. I took two choruses, the same as Prez. I could have done more, but I liked what I said. If two choruses were good enough for Prez, they were good enough for me.

When we finished, they applauded, really applauded. I was basking in the glow when the girl in red pushed through from the kitchen with Horace in tow. Not only her lip but her whole cheek was puffed up. Horace didn't have a mark on him, except for his spacey eyes.

Horace opened his mouth, but nothing was coming out. She nudged him in the ribs.

"Sorry," he mumbled.

She nudged him.

"Sorry I...."

Nudge.

"...I'm such a ugly asshole."

"No!" she screamed. "You're not ugly! You're not ugly, and you're not a, a, a hatemonger! You just think you are, but I know you're not, you're just.... you're just a teddy bear!"

She put both arms around him, burying her fat-lipped swollen face in his chest and starting to cry. He looked up for a spacey instant, as if to God. Then he started hauling her to the door.

We played a couple more sets, throwing in some extra time because we were late. About 12:45 we packed up, got our money, said goodbye to Al, and got on the freeway. George lit up a joint and passed it around.

"So Artie," said Reuben. "Were you really going to kick that guy's ass?"

"'Spook.' 'Nigger music.' I was going to kill the son of a bitch."

"You know," I said, "I don't think he knew what a diatribe was. Probably thought it was a bunch of Indians."

Artie giggled. "These guys panic when they hear a word they don't know."

"Weird gig," said George. "Bodies on the freeway. Pussy-whipped Klansman. Weird."

"Good thing his girl friend was there. And that guy Al," said Reuben.

"Wasn't she something," I said. "How does a guy like him get a girl like her? Where did she come from anyway? Born-again Christian with an ACLU conscience? Thinks he's a teddy bear?"

"Maybe he isn't all that bad," said Reuben. "Maybe it's like she said, he thinks he's ugly and dumb and is just grabbing at scapegoats."

"*Just,*" said Artie. "That's a big word, *just.* Just keep him away from me. But she was definitely some kind of alien mutant, bless her heart."

The joint got handed back to George. He took a huge toke.

"Well," he croaked, after about an hour, letting out a blast of dope-heavy breath just before he turned blue in the face. "One thing is for sure. The guy just wasn't professional."

Nobody could argue with that.

HOMECOMING

It was Brander, the chaplain's assistant and his own tent mate, who broke the news to him.

"You're a-goin' home, ol' buddy. You got to kiss all these-here gook gals *gooo*-bye."

He had kissed only one hello, the B-girl he'd groped on the stairs to her dance-hall. Brander, on the other hand, was the company's major womanizer. As chaplain's assistant, he had virtually unlimited use of the chaplain's weapons carrier, and he knew what to do with it in a war-blasted city like Manila, where the streets were mostly mud and girls were easy to pick up. Once, struggling to thread a needle to sew a pocket on his fatigues that had been nearly ripped off by one of his women, he had chuckled, "Put hair on it and I wun't have no trouble." How he had become a chaplain's assistant was beyond Richard's ken. Obviously he had to be as hypocritical as he was sexually depraved, but was the chaplain that obtuse? Or that depraved himself?

Richard had never actually met the chaplain, as he didn't attend services. Once, late one moonlit night, courting a spiritual experience, he had visited the empty chapel, which was an open-air shelter made of local bamboo. Nothing happened. Or maybe, he thought, the non-happening was itself a spiritual experience, just being there alone, in the moonlight.

As for going home, it turned out Brander was right. In two weeks he was to be flown home. The reason was that his brother Stanton had been killed in the last days of the war in Europe, and it seemed the army had a policy that families who had lost one son should not be at peril of losing another. The policy had not prevented them from shipping him overseas as infantry replacement in the first place, but if they wanted to ship him stateside now, he was willing.

Not that he was in any peril, sitting at company headquarters typing out morning reports, thanks to Mr. Moseby, his junior high typing teacher. When he had first arrived ten months earlier, a month after the dropping of the atomic bombs on Hiroshima and Nagasaki, there had been idiots on the troop train, fired up with the rotgut liquor hawked by the natives at every stop, talking about going up in the hills to hunt for Japs. They rather frightened Richard. Saved by the nuclear incineration of a gazillion civilians from the suicidal storming of the beaches of Japan, they wanted to risk their lives hunting Japs who hadn't heard the war was over? He was too inexperienced to know that that was the rotgut talking.

The closest Richard had been to combat was when the lieutenant in charge of Headquarters Company decided that the Filipinos who worked on the base, pulling weeds, doing laundry, were stealing too much government property, mainly the mess gears which they filled at the garbage cans at mess hall, retrieving for their families the leftovers that the GIs scraped off their metal trays. Probably the mess gear had not been stolen but given to them by GIs, who had no need for them. But the law-and-order lieutenant had ordered him, loaded carbine at ready, to stand at the gate to the compound, while inside the gate, the locals leaving for the day were ordered to throw their mess gear, filled or unfilled, on a pile as they filed out. They hesitantly relinquished the gear, but instead of filing out, they stepped nervously back, forming an ever-growing crowd silently watching as the ones in line behind them threw their gear on the pile and joined them. Finally, one woman, having just, very reluctantly, laid her mess gear on the pile, suddenly turned, grabbed back her mess gear, and ran. Immediately the whole crowd did the same, the pile of mess gear diminishing to a few scattered knives and forks in a matter of seconds. Richard, standing with carbine at ready, heard no order from the exasperated, pistol-waving lieutenant, and could not have used any kind of force if he had.

He did not immediately write his parents that he was coming home. In fact, the more he thought about it, the more he liked the idea of arriving home unannounced, delivering to his parents a joyous surprise.

Things at home had changed, he knew. After his brother's death his parents, though still struggling with his mother's nervous breakdown, had agreed to be guardians to a 16-year-old juvenile delinquent who had gotten in trouble for an attempted warehouse robbery in which a security guard had been severely beaten. According to Clifford's parents, the young man, named Dan, had not been involved in the beating, being posted as a lookout. But in the course of their guardianship, while living in Richard's old room, Dan had revealed himself as a poor candidate for rehabilitation, ignoring their rules, staying out late, smoking in Richard's bed, being surly at the dinner table. One day Richard's mother, breaking her own rule about respecting Dan's privacy as she would have repected that of her own sons, found in his room a Prince Albert tobacco tin containing what she thought, correctly, was marijuana; a hammer with one tapered, pointed end, a type used by burglars; a black jack, shaped like a six-inch baseball bat and filled at the big end with lead; and a set of brass knuckles. The brass knuckles especially horrified her. A boy who would use brass knuckles did not belong in their home, and they returned Dan to the custody of juvenile court.

More recently, Richard's parents had been introduced by musical friends to Lyle, a brilliant young pianist from Iowa, now a student at USC, who needed a place to live. Their last letter had been full of warm appreciation of Lyle, though they wanted to discuss it with Richard before actually taking him in.

Richard had a vague sense that his parents, devastated by the death of Stanton, were attempting to replace him. Dan had been a mistake, a hard case who saw his parents' compassion as weakness. But Lyle was a different matter, a musical achiever like Stanton, who had fulfilled all his parents' dreams.

As the younger son, the baby of the family, he knew he had been his mother's favorite, but as the son who merely tolerated her, who had quit piano to take up swing drumming, and who spent every minute not practicing paradiddles and ratamacues shooting hoops on the basketball court, he knew he was a disappointment. Just before going into the army, tiring of drums, he had taken clarinet lessons from a friend of Stanton's, and he had even bought a used saxophone, with visions of playing like Coleman Hawkins, whose recording of "Body and Soul" he had just discovered. But he knew he could not take Stanton's place, and his parents' involvement with Dan and now Lyle was understandable. Yet he had misgivings.

He was comforted by visions of his joyous homecoming. He would have flowers sent, and after they arrived with their message of filial love and proximity, he would be on the doorstep in person. He had confided his plan to Mickey, the company medic whose pet spider-monkey always rode on his shoulder, and Mickey had told him about a cousin in the Marines who had come home unannounced at four in the morning. His mother, in her nightgown, answered his knock, let out a joyous whoop, and threw her arms around him. The whole family came running, and they all celebrated with an early breakfast of pancakes, bacon, and eggs.

Richard's military plane would arrive in Long Beach at 8:30 A.M., on a Saturday, so there would be no need to get his parents out of bed in the wee hours. He could order the flowers in Long Beach, and by the time he got to Glendale they would have arrived in time for his grand entrance.

On the plane, drowsing, remembering the night at the chapel, he found himself taking stock, spiritually and otherwise. What was this surprise package he was bringing to his parents?

Physically, he knew, he was in excellent shape. Unlike Stanton, he had always been athletic. Besides playing freshman football and varsity basketball, he had taken boxing classes in high school, had thought about fighting as an amateur, and on the troop ship coming over he had been the heavyweight champion. Only four had signed up for the tournament, so it was no big deal. But still, he had won his two fights. He could have knocked the second guy out, but, seeing the opening, he had pulled the punch, not wanting to hurt him. On base there was no gym, only an asphalt basketball court, of which he made daily use. But behind the screen at the outdoor stage where they showed movies, the technician in charge, Sergeant Capella, had installed a couple of heavy bags and a light punching bag. A slightly built man, balding, with a beaky, rodent-like, heavily creased face, he had fought pro as a bantamweight in the clubs of Brooklyn, his home town. The bags, he said, were there for whoever wanted to use them, but Richard never saw anyone else who did. When Sarge saw that Richard was interested, he began training him, showing him how to use the bags, how to shadow-box, how to use his feet, how to throw a left hook, how to put together combinations: jab, right cross, left hook, uppercut. The sweet science, he said. Sweet not in the punches landed, they were not sweet, guys got punch-drunk or killed, but sweet in the punches evaded, in making the guy with the big punch look like a fool, sweet in the science of it, like Billy Conn with Joe Louis, making it look easy not to get killed. Until Louis caught up to him. Sarge would shake his head and look up with a slanty little grin. But everyone does, he would say, get killed, don't they? Conn, he put it off for thirteen rounds. Pretty good, sweet.

Unknown to Richard, others had been working out with Sarge, enough to form a boxing team, and one day Sarge told him they were having a tourney with the Blackhawk division, and that he was to be part of it. Not to worry, he would fight another novice.

The fight itself was kind of fun. Neither he nor his opponent landed a single good punch. What Sarge hadn't taught him was how to rush a back-pedaling opponent to get close enough to hit him. After all the fights were over, he and his opponent, named Neil, had drinks in the company bar.

"Man," said Neil, "when I saw you, how well you were built, all those muscles, I knew I was in trouble. You nearly nailed me, a couple of times."

"I was scared to death," said Richard, which was not exactly true; he was nervous, yes, but not really scared.

"How long you been boxing," said Neil.

"Since high school, I took it for gym."

"You must have had all kinds of girls chasing after you," said Neil.

"Not really," Richard admitted, sheepishly. He had struck out with girls in high school. They scared him, especially the pretty ones.

"Hard to believe," said Neil.

Richard excused himself to go to the rest room. As he stood urinating, Neil was suddenly behind him, on his knees.

"Let me do you, give me your cock, I love you," he was saying.

Richard stumbled past him, almost knocking him over with his knee. Running to his tent, he fell in a muddy ditch he normally jumped over. *What was wrong with him*, he thought, rising from the mud. He had been brought up to sympathize with the underdog--the poor, Negroes, even homosexuals. But now the queers thought he was one of them. Was he queer too?

The episode with the B-girl had somewhat assuaged his anxiety on that score. Brander and he had picked her up in the weapons carrier. A bright-eyed, dimpled, breast-flaunting little dumpling of a girl, she had excited a physical passion he had never known. On the stairs to her dance hall, kissing him, breathing in his ear, she had offered herself for $30, a month's take-home pay he did not have. He did not even have the money to follow her into the dance hall. As she twisted from his embrace to go to work, she had suddenly giggled and grabbed his swollen penis, setting off an orgasm that exploded even as he ran, in fear for his life, from the knife-wielding bouncer at the top of the stairs.

Back in the weapons carrier, waiting for Brander, covering himself, dreading Brander's hilarity if he found out that Richard had come in his pants, he dreaded even more the likelihood that Brander, if he knew, would insist on pursuing the girl at the dance hall. He felt a sudden revulsion at what he had done, at what his life could become if he followed Brander's path. Neither of his parents, they had told him, had had sex before their marriage, and they had recently sent him a diplomatically worded letter hoping that he would resist the temptations that soldiers in foreign lands were naturally prey to. As Brander came running toward him in the rain that had just started, he felt he had come perilously close to losing his character.

Now, on the plane, it was not the B-girl he thought about but another girl. One night several of them had gone in the weapons carrier to a dance at a Knights of Columbus hall and picked up some women. On the way to the weapons carrier the one he was with, a slender girl with serious, intelligent eyes, had suddenly squatted in the parking lot to urinate. In the weapons carrier, he put his arm around her, feeling that she was a person of substance, unlike the B-girl. It had taken a certain courage to squat and urinate like that, in defiance of etiquette. Then, as the weapons carrier slowed to turn at a muddy corner, she broke from him, muttering something negative, and jumped out. Poised at the tailgate, he felt the impulse to jump after her. But he did not know where he was or how he would get back to the base, and so he did not jump. But she remained in his mind as a real person, someone he might have cared about.

The bounce as the plane hit the runway on landing woke him. Stepping out of the plane into a typically balmy, foggy June morning in Long Beach, he remembered with a little thrill the smell of those mornings--sea air, fog, exhaust fumes, orange blossoms. He was home.

According to plan, he found a phone in the terminal, looked up a florist shop he remembered in Glendale, and called to order his flowers. There was no answer. Apparently the plane had come in early, and the shop was not yet open. With his duffle bag hanging from his shoulder, he caught a taxi to where he could board the red car to Los Angeles and Glendale. The ride itself, with all the windows open, was delicious, up through the truck farms of Bellflower and Downey to Terminal Annex and finally Brand Boulevard, where the flower shop was. By now it was almost noon. The shop was open, and he ordered his flowers. When would they be delivered? The girl at the counter looked at her watch. The delivery boy had called in sick, and the owner was out to lunch and wouldn't be back till one or one-thirty. So probably they wouldn't be able to deliver the flowers until around two.

So he had two hours to kill. He could go to a bar. He was not yet twenty-one, but because of the uniform they would probably serve him. Sitting on a bar stool for two hours, however, did not appeal to him. The main library, where he had spent some hours in high school researching a term paper on jazz, was nearby, but he felt too jittery for that. It occurred to him that his old basketball buddy Wayne's house was only a mile from his own. Wayne was still in the navy, but his parents were pretty sure to be home on a Saturday afternoon. He could go there and wait until the flower shop called to tell him the flowers were delivered. He had forgotten Wayne's phone number, but he looked it up and gave it to the girl at the flower ship, with instructions to call him there when they had delivered the flowers. He did not call Wayne's parents. He preferred to walk there, sure that they would be home.

His assumption was correct. Properly amazed to see him, Wayne's parents invited him in. How long had he been back? How were his parents? Why was he carrying his duffle bag? As he was explaining how he had not been home yet but was waiting for the flower shop to deliver the flowers and call, Wayne's father, a lawyer, excused himself and left the room.

"It's a surprise," said Richard. "They don't know. They think I'm still in the Philippines."

"You didn't tell them you were coming home?" said Wayne's mother.

"No. They haven't heard from me for three weeks."

"Oh my. They will be surprised. Maybe we ought to drive you home right now?"

"The flower shop is supposed to call," he said. "There'll be a card with the flowers. If you could drive me then, it would be great."

"Yes, of course."

"How's Wayne?"

"He's in Nevada now. A navy training school on Lake Mead," said his mother. "Near the Grand Canyon. He loves it."

As he recalled Wayne's outdoorsman proclivities—they had once gone deep sea fishing together, driving recklessly through thick pre-dawn fog to San Pedro--the doorbell rang and Wayne's father reappeared to answer it. When he opened the door, Richard's own father entered the room.

"Daddy," said Richard, standing up.

In younger days his father's socialist friends said he looked like Trotsky, with his mustache and wild black hair. But he had never had Trotsky's bellicose set of jaw or fiery agitator's eyes. His father's eyes were kind, but with dark hollows under them, darker, Richard thought, than before.

His father hugged him.

"Welcome home, welcome home, son."

"Did the flowers come?" said Richard.

"Flowers?"

"I sent you flowers, with a card. That's why I came here, to wait for the flowers to come, so you'd know I was home. I wanted to surprise you. Does Mother know I'm here?"

"No, she was playing when Mr. Wickham called. We're actually in the middle of a recital we're having, for Lyle. You remember we told you about Lyle?"

"He's there now?"

"At the recital, yes. He and his friend Eddie are a two-piano team, and we bought another piano, an old upright, not too expensive. Lyle likes it."

Mrs. Wickham, who had left the room, now reentered with a tray of cookies.

"Lyle," she said brightly. "Your other son? How good it will be now to have them both home."

"No, no," said Richard's father, staring at Mrs. Wickham, whom he had never met, with anguished eyes. "Stanton. Stanton was our other son. We lost him."

"In the war," said Richard. "He was killed in the war." Saying it, he felt strange, as if he had left his body.

"I'm so sorry," said Mrs. Wickham, her hand over her mouth. "I didn't know."

"Lyle," said his father, trying to put her at ease, "is a young pianist we have taken an interest in. We're having a little musical gathering for him."

"And I'm sure you want to get back to it, with your prodigal son here," said Mr. Wickham. He took Richard's hand in both of his, shaking it briskly.

"And you, Mr. Surprise," he said, "welcome home."

"Thank you for calling," his father said to Wickham, his hand on Richard's elbow, leading him out the door.

"But the flowers," Richard began, then realized it was too late, his mother would get no advance warning.

The tinny old four-cylinder Willys, still the family car, waited at the curb. Settling himself in the passenger seat, Richard recalled the night he had taken Caroline Stevens to a movie in it. He had lost his temper, when, parked outside her parents' expensive house in the hills, she had snatched the keys and initiated a game of keepaway with him. Somehow, his embarrassment about the Willys, which everyone considered a joke of a car, had entered into his inability to play what he later realized was a game meant to bring them into physical contact.

"Your mother," said his father as they reached the house, "is not very strong these days. You know she had that nervous breakdown, and her ulcer is still acting up. I think I had better go in first to prepare her. You wait on the porch."

As Richard stood on the porch, duffle bag slung from his shoulder, he could hear the sound of two pianos. Bach, it sounded like. They were good, very good. Then, with the two pianos still playing, the door opened, and his mother was there, crying, embracing him, kissing him on the mouth. Her hair was as it had always been, two long braids coiled around the top of her head. She had never set foot in a beauty shop or tried to do her hair any other way.

"We were so worried when we didn't hear from you," she was saying.

"I'm sorry. I should have written. I thought...."

"And you went first to Wayne's house. Oh Richard," she wailed, kissing him again.

"That was so the flowers would come first. I tried to order them in Long Beach, but the flower shop wasn't open...."

The two-piano music had stopped. There was applause. His mother pulled him into the hall. There were fifteen or twenty people on rented folding chairs in the living room. The two pianists, Lyle, whom he recognized from a snapshop his parents had sent him, and the man he assumed was Eddie stood by the pianos, Lyle's fair, gracefully wavy hair contrasting with Eddie's mop of tight black curls. His mother clapped her hands for silence.

"We have a great surprise. Our son is home from overseas."

Our other, our un-dead son, thought Richard, to enthusiastic applause. Apparently the recital was over. People stood and milled about. Some he knew as his mother's piano students or parents of students. Frances Vosbein, his father's buxom fat-cheeked co-worker at the Food for All Foundation, gave him a robust bear hug. Dr. Lovejoy, his father's oldest friend from their boyhood in Kansas, and his wife Betty and daughter Adelaide, prettier and more grown-up than he remembered, filed by to shake his hand.

"And this," said his mother, leading Lyle by the elbow, "is Lyle, who we wrote you about. Doesn't he play beautifully?"

Lyle's handshake was a trifle limp.

"Yes, he does," he mumbled. "I only heard a little bit."

"Your mother," said Lyle, "says you like jazz. Would you like to hear some now?"

"You play jazz?"

"Does he ever," said Eddie, joining them. "He takes Art Tatum solos off the records."

Richard had three prized Art Tatum records. He could hardly imagine the skill required to learn a Tatum solo off the record, by ear.

"Name a song," said Lyle.

"'Body and Soul'?"

"I don't believe Tatum has recorded that song, but I'll try to play it as he might," said Lyle, seating himself at the baby grand.

The rippling runs and arpeggios were exactly in the Tatum style. Richard was awed and humbled. If Lyle and Eddie were a pair of homosexuals, what did it matter? To be able to play like that. His own vague notion of taking up piano again seemed utterly futile.

"How do you do that?" he asked. But he knew how, by practicing, as Stanton had, instead of shooting baskets on the playground. He felt it was the stupidest thing in the world that he had quit piano.

"I understand you used to play piano," said Lyle, smiling at his mother, "and I think your mother would like you to start again."

"Yes," said his mother, "she certainly would."

"It's too late," said Richard.

"Not really," said Lyle. "You're still young, and you're athletic. Part of it is just a form of athleticism, training muscles, reflexes."

"Maybe on saxophone," said Richard.

"Do you have one? It's true, one note at a time is easier than piano."

His mother started guiltily, fingers to her lips.

"Oh dear, Richard, I'm so sorry, we had to sell it. Arthur was between jobs, we needed the money for food, to pay the mortgage, and the doctor bills. Now that Arthur is with the Foundation, we could shop for another one."

"Maybe," said Richard. He felt suddenly quite tired. "Could I be excused? I've been up a long time, with the plane flight and all."

"Oh dear," said his mother, looking guilty again. "There are no sheets on your bed. If we had known you were coming...."

"It's okay. I'm so tired it won't matter."

He shook hands with Lyle and Eddie and gave his mother the kiss she was demanding, not, he made sure this time, on the mouth.

His room upstairs was basically the same, the worn green and white linoleum on the floor, cracked at the edges, the blue-striped single-bed mattress with urine stains, the bed-springs that squeaked when he sat down. His record player was on the table at the foot of the bed, in front of the bookcase with his records.

Beside the record player were objects he didn't recognize at first: a hammer with a long pointed rat-tail opposite the head, a miniature baseball bat filled with lead, a metal contraption he didn't recognize. Dan's things, he realized with a start. Of course. He couldn't have taken them back to juvenile lock-up, and his parents had just left them on the table.

He tried on the brass knuckles, made a fist, inspected the lead-filled black jack, hefted the long-tailed burglar's hammer. They were his now, whatever that meant. Nothing, presumably, unless Dan were really his evil twin. He leafed through a record album. Coleman Hawins on Bluebird label, Roy Eldridge and Lester Young on

Commodore, Don Byas on National. He put Lester's "Way Down Yonder in New Orleans," where he played clarinet, on the record player and lay back, listening. Lester was so beautiful. He himself couldn't play anything anymore, not flute, not piano, not drums, not clarinet. His saxophone was gone. Stanton, who could have helped him, was dead. Now there was this Lyle. Maybe he would call Caroline Stevens, see if she was married or what.

HIGHER EDUCATION

Clifford, a senior at Demeter College, was looking forward to his father's visit. He had always loved his father more than his mother, even as a child. Tucking him in at night, his father would run his fingers through his hair, and scratch the top of his head, and read him poems about Wynken, Blynken, and Nod, or the little sick mouse who missed his geraniums red, delphiniums blue. When he kissed him goodnight, his whiskers against his neck would tickle and make him laugh.

He had always called him Daddy, but he learned in the army not to. In a late night bull session about sex, he had volunteered that his daddy had taught him to wait until he was married, and one of the group had sneered, "Your *daddy!* He calls his old man *daddy!*"

Now, speaking to others, he referred to him as "my father," but in direct address he did not know what name to use. He could not bring himself to address him as "Dad." When his father arrived, Clifford would simply say "Hi" and shake his hand.

Clifford no longer believed it necessary to put off sex till after marriage. Yet he remained a virgin, and he still, after all the years of high school and the army, had never had a steady girl friend. He might perhaps have changed all that the other night, when Angie, a pretty freshman, had come unbidden to his off-campus room. He had been lying on the floor, a gallon of cheap red wine at his side and one of Beethoven's last quartets, Opus 132, coursing through him at high volume from his record player, when he heard someone knock. He was astonished to see her. In company with his friend Markham they had sipped coffee at the Co-op, but pretty as she was, he had not taken her quite seriously. Now that she was standing on his doorstep, he did not, half drunk, rightly know what to do. They ended up lying side-by-side on the floor, drinking wine and listening to Opus 32. He was not disposed, at this point, to convert this communion via wine and Beethoven into a physical encounter. Really, he hardly knew her. Besides, she had to be back at her dorm by 10.

He learned later that Markham had put her up to it, told her where he lived. What else had he told her? Markham had read Freud and was undergoing psychoanalysis. He had loaned Clifford *A General Introduction to Psychoanalysis* and a psychoanalyst's interpretation of Coleridge which made much of the poet's "latent homosexualilty." Had Markham told her of Clifford's concerns about his own love life, or lack thereof? Of his visit to Markham's psychoanalyst? Clifford had not asked.

He planned to tell his father about the visit to Markham's analyst. For one thing, if he were to go into analysis himself, he would need more money than his GI benefits provided. For another, although he had never confided in his father about personal problems and had no idea how to go about it, in his present state he felt he needed his love and support, which had always been unconditional.

There were many things, of course, that he could never tell his father. He could not tell him of getting drunk in the company bar, of the time he fell in a shallow ditch on the way back to his tent, bellowing to his drinking mates that he couldn't get up.

Nor would he tell his father of the time a group of them had driven 50 miles in the chaplain's assistant's weapons carrier to a whorehouse, a frond-roofed shack in the jungle. He had not wanted to go but was unable to resist the group pressure. When they had all entered and seated themselves, waiting their turns, he had found himself shaking, in a cold sweat, terrified beyond any fear he had ever experienced. He could not possibly have gone behind a screen with one of those skinny, probably syphilitic girls. While he was imagining total impotence, the madam announced that she could not accomodate them, because the Military Police had shut them down. And so he had been able, after all, to keep his promise to his parents, made in a recent letter, that he would preserve his virginity for marriage.

He had not, in that letter, mentioned his masturbation, which he had practiced in pre- and then post-puberty forms almost nightly, from the time he was four. By his parents, his early masturbation was called "gouging his q-ter." "Q-ter was what they called his penis, instead of the common "P-ter." When he urinated, he did not "pee," he "qued."

The term "gouging" came from his method, which his mother had made him describe: he would lie on his stomach, hands clasped under his upturned penis, and gyrate his hips. He had promised his mother that he would quit when he advanced to first grade. He could not keep that promise, even after she caught him several times at nap time and whipped him on his bare legs with a cherry-tree switch, he howling and dancing and begging her to stop. It was only after he had come home from the army and been subjected by the Veteran's Administration to a psychological test, in order to qualify for his educational benefits, that his mind had been at some ease about masturbation.

His test, according to the examiner, had shown a high "lie quotient." As honesty was something on which he prided himself, he was shocked. It seemed that the key questions had to do with masturbation, which he had admitted to, and "sexual perversion," which he had also admitted to. The examiner had explained to him that masturbation was not considered a perversion.

None of this had entered into his initial conversation with Markham's analyst, Dr. Miller. Why had he come, the doctor wanted to know. Clifford told him that he had always had difficulty approaching women, and when he read the book Markham had given him, about Coleridge's latent homosexualilty, it made him anxious that perhaps he was a latent homosexual, that maybe that was the reason he had such difficultly even asking women out. And sometimes other men would approach him, like Harold Diefenbocker at school, who came to his room and talked about how lonely he was, and how he, Clifford, seemed like such a sensitive person, and he hoped they could be friends. Clifford had felt uneasy, sensing that probably Diefenbocker was homosexual, and was trying to find out if Clifford was also. But he had endured Diefenbocker, conversationally, for the evening, because he knew no way out of his discomfort without hurting Diefenbocker's feelings. He had always felt sorry for homosexuals. Prejudice against them was as cruel and unfair as prejudice against Negroes, and he would not use words like "queer" and "faggot." But why were homosexuals like Diefenbocker attracted to him?

"Have you ever been sexually attracted to a male?" Dr. Miller asked.

If Clifford knew one thing, it was that he had felt desire only for women. But why, he asked, had he never had one?

"There are many possible reasons," said Dr. Miller drily, "other than latent homosexuality."

The rest of the session had been largely devoted to the question of whether Clifford could afford to be psychoanalyzed. Obviously, he could not, without his parents' help. Dr. Miller had suggested that "maturation," over time, might solve his problems. Clifford found that prospect singularly unattractive.

As had been arranged, he met his father at the Edgemont Inn, a venerable brown-shingle institution just at the edge of campus. He had never eaten at the Edgemont, and would never have done so had his father not been there to pay the bill. Aside from the expense, its gentility was a formidable deterrent. Clifford perferred Lupe's, on the highway, where drama majors and other literary types drank their beer in pitchers. He was himself a literary type, in awe of Joyce and Faulkner and Hemingway.

At lunch his father conveyed to him that his mother's migraines were acting up again, as they had intermittently ever since Clifford's older brother had been killed in the war. And as executive secretary of No More Hunger, a non-profit relief organization, his father was very busy getting out an appeal for aid to victims of a recent earthquake in India.

"How are your classes?" asked his father. "What exactly are you taking?"

"Romanticism, Shakespeare, Lit Crit."

"Litcrit?"

"Literary Criticism. Actually that's the best one. We did Aristotle's *Poetics*, and *Oedipus Rex*. Then we read a Freudian interpretation of *Hamlet*. I'm writing a paper on that."

His father removed his horn-rim glasses and put the tip of one frame-arm between his front teeth.

"And what is the Freudian interpretation of *Hamlet?*"

"Well," said Clifford, trying not to stammer, "it has to do with the Oedipus complex. You know the story?"

"Of the play, *Oedipus*? I must have read it at some time. And of course, like most people, I've heard about Freud and the Oedipus complex. But tell me."

"Well, in the story Oedipus kills his father and marries his mother, without knowing it. Who they are, I mean. Freud says all male children unconsciously want to, um, get rid of their father and marry their mother, have her all to themselves. But society won't allow this, so males have to repress everything, and Freud calls this the Oedipus complex. Hamlet really wanted to do what his uncle actually did, and that's why he can't bring himself to avenge his father's murder by killing his uncle, because he feels guilty for having the same desires as his uncle. In a sense Hamlet actually has two fathers, his real one, the ghost, and his imagined one, and...."

Observing his father bemusedly shaking his head, he stopped.

"How does one," said his father, with a quizzical half-smile, "unconsciously want something? If you want something, you want it. Or are you talking about a split personality?"

"Not exactly. But in a way, everyone's a split personality. We have these hidden desires, things we want that we can't admit to, forbidden things. Freud has this whole theory of the unconscious...."

"So Hamlet is a split personality?" His father sighed. "It seems to me that you don't require a split personality or an Oedipus complex to explain why Hamlet is disturbed that his uncle murdered his father, or why he is angry with his mother for marrying his uncle, or why Hamlet can't bring himself to execute him, as he is expected to do. All decent people would find that hard."

His father, Clifford knew, opposed capital punishment. He believed in rehabilitation, in giving murderers a chance to repent of their crimes. In every man there was the possibility of good.

"I guess so. But Hamlet's main worry is whether his uncle is really guilty or not. And anyway, the big scene with his mother, where he's so obsessed with her lust... "

His father waved his hand dismissively, his large-nosed, normally kindly face darkened by an impatient frown. It was a gesture Clifford had seen often, usually in his father's exasperated response to his mother during some trivial dispute.

"I still don't see any need for Freud. Lust is lust, it doesn't need an Oedipus complex to make it real."

Clifford shrugged, hiding his disappointment.

"It's just a theory. But what we read," he went on, determined to salvage something for Freud, "was really interesting. That's why I decided to write a paper about it."

His father smiled encouragingly and patted his shoulder. "I'm sure you'll do a good one."

Their lunch ended, they left the Edgemont and strolled toward Clifford's room. In front of the library they encountered Markham and Angie. With some anxiety, Clifford introduced his father. His anxiety was due, in part, to Markham's unpredictability--he was surprised to see him emerging from the library, as Markham seldom spent much time there--and in part to a concern as to how his father would react to Markham's imposing physical presence. Markham was 6'3", and Clifford, who at 6'2" was three inches taller than his father, always felt the impulse to step backward when face to face with Markham, whose massive head felt like a boulder about to fall on him.

His father stood his ground. "Happy to meet you. Are you English majors also?"

"Yes and no," said Markham. "Cliff and I are partners in crime, but Angie here is just a freshman. She doesn't know what to do with her life yet."

"Neither do you," laughed Angie. "You don't even know what to do with your courses.." Markham, a lazy student, was flunking both Romanticism and Lit Crit because of not turning in papers. "And all Cliff wants to do," added Angie unexpectedly, "is lie around listening to Beethoven quartets."

His father, a clarinetist who had played professionally in younger days, turned to him, pleased at Clifford's choice of music. "Beethoven quartets?"

"The last ones," said Clifford, alarmed yet secretly pleased by Angie's covert reference to the other night. "I just discovered them."

"But rest assured," interjected Markham, smiling broadly, his small squinty eyes glinting, "he is not neglecting his studies for Beethoven. Clifford here is the star of our Lit Crit class, the master of the intricate Freudian interpretation of *Hamlet*."

"Yes," said his father, "he was telling me about that." He looked at his watch. "I'm afraid I have to get back to the city. It's been a pleasure meeting you both." He shook hands with Markham and Angie, and he and Clifford continued their progress toward Clifford's room.

"That was nice," said his father, "meeting your friends. Angie is a very pretty girl."

With some pride, Clifford said, unthinkingly, "She came to my room last night."

His father's face darkened alarmingly.

"Never betray a woman's indiscretions," he said, staring straight ahead, jaw firmly clenched.

Stunned, Clifford groped for a response. It was true. Angie had been indiscreet, and he had told his father, out of pride. He could not remember his father's ever rebuking him in this way, but he deserved it. He had behaved dishonorably. But not as dishonorably as his father was assuming.

"Nothing happened," he blurted. "We listened to Beethoven."

His father's expression softened. Then, uncomfortably, he asked, "Are you still a virgin?"

Ashamed of his answer, Clifford stammered: "Y-y-yes."

They had reached Clifford's room, in the back of a private home. At the door his father embraced him.

"Mother and I love you, Clifford. You seem to be going through a phase. We want you to be happy. If you need any help...."

"I do. I've been to see Markham's analyst, but he's expensive. I thought...."

"Markham's *analyst*? *Psychoanalyst?* Why didn't you come to me? Why didn't you come to Eckhardt, or Frank Stone, or Albert?"

Eckhart, a recent acquaintance of his father's, was a handwriting analyst for the Los Angeles Police Department. Frank Stone was an eminent family psychologist his father had known since childhood. Albert was Albert Lake, his father's closest friend, his colleague in political muckraking in earlier years. Growing up, Clifford had sat entranced through countless political discussions with Albert.

"Daddy, they're not psychoanalysts."

"Psychoanalysis! Freud!" exclaimed his father. "Everything reduced to sex! What matters is not sex, not Oedipus wanting to kill his father and marry his mother, not studying your own belly button! Compassion, service to others, that's where you'll find yourself, not psychoanalysis!"

Before Clifford could answer, his father turned angrily on his heel and strode down the driveway. Watching his receding back, Clifford saw his future bearing down, on iron rails. He knew he should call out, or run to his father, but could only stand and watch as he rounded the hedged corner of the driveway and disappeared.

POEMS

TRAVELING

You're in a hotel,
you've been there for days
and it's time to pay the bill.
You should have paid it day by day,
but no one told you, and now
the manager is angry, perhaps
he will not take your money,
if you have it, as perhaps
you don't. You look in your wallet.
It's stuffed with banknotes
and rainchecks from the market,
but the currency is wrong, somehow,
and you go out into the street
and are immediately lost,
trying to get back, wondering,
as you wander the muddy roads,
why you ever left home, and how
you could have been allowed not to.

FOR LESTER YOUNG

Listening to Lester,
thinking of you listening too,
the music a key to a hidden room
seldom entered, except
when two hear on the wind
the same lowered voice
(that is not this voice)
the same strange sad story
(that is not this story)
the same love-wrenched tune
(that is not this tune)
but is somewhere
just the other side
of time.

A TALK WITH A CROW

A crow flew down
from a phone pole.
It was black, black,
sitting there on
the barbecue.

I said, "You know,
you look just like
I feel. Like shit."

"Poor boy," he said,
"Is your little heart
breaking some?
In two? In three,
or four?
"Yeah," I said,
my gal done left me."

"I know just how
you feel," he said.
"My gal left me

Safford Chamberlain

Once. Flew over
a corn field, got
shot all to hell.
She learned her lesson,
you bet. Haw, haw!"

"And your heart
was broken, right?"

"Shit no. I got
me another gal.
Plenty of crows
in the sky."

"Well,"
I said, "women
are different.
"This one I knew

could laugh and cuss
and open doors. If
you spit on the windshield
to wash it, she wouldn't even
blink. Sometimes
she talked like a crow
about love and the
weather. She could

cock her head sideways
too, just like you,
and make the world

tilt. You just can't
pick that kind
out of the sky."

"You poor dumb bastard,"
he said. "I didn't think
there were any like
you left in this
fucking world. But here,
she told me to
give you this crow's eye."

I looked through it
as he flapped away,
and the world tilted.

PROFESSOR CROW
GIVES A LECTURE

"The conversation of crows is wholly about love and the weather."

---Attributed to Homer

I see, dear boy, you are consumed
with bitterness and rancor. You
forget, it seems, those simple rules
of decent thought that you were taught
by your good Daddy. And when
your new love you revile
with words like bitch and cunt,
when you her curse, you smudge
with smut your Daddy's soul, who knew
that self must suffer and forbear,
must give up every cherished grudge
to hope to breathe love's stunning air.

AT THE BUS STOP: A HISTORY

At a New Year's party
they celebrated their disengagement.
She threw a drink in some guy's face,
and next day hitchhiked to Berkeley,
narrowly escaping rape by a truck driver.

Reconciling on the beach in Ventura,
they smoked Mary Jane's Mary Jane,
and as the full moon rose,
time stopped. Turning around,
he learned the difference
between north and south,
light and dark.

Now, after a weekend
in Berkeley, in her hayloft room
with the big barn door window,
he was leaving her, loving her, again,
waiting in fog for the bus,
when this kid, her classmate, comes up,
nervy, hitting on her,

the bus getting closer,
engine rising in a whine
and dying at each stop.

The kid won't go away,
and no one tells him to.

APHRODITE ABSCONDITUS

One evening, as I groaned to think myself
corrupt, my clenched eyes were touched by lips
that spoke, gently battering with moist breath
my eyelids: "Good friend, do not despair. I too
have loved the flesh too much. I know those bleak
couplings, the looming nil,
the tide that drowns all kisses.
I have come to show you my wound, to finger
yours, to let them bleed into each other
as speech answers speech in the time
before tongues, hands, bellies sink
in the bestial dark.
For this is love, my friend,
this is the beautful.
Will you let me share your grief?"
I groaned again, this time for joy,
but when I opened my eyes there was only
the waiting dark. Had I dreamed
or been merely lied to? She was a bitch,
it seems. Yet her lies were the lies of a goddess.

DEPOSITION, RE THE MATTER OF ABRAHAM AND ISAAC

That's right, I told him to.
I knew he doted on him, loved
the shit in his stinking diapers,
so how better to test his loyalty
than by making him murder
the dear brat? I needed him
to tie the kid up, and lay him
on the stack of sticks,
and kneel, and weep, and pray,
and hold the knife to his throat.
But hey, I didn't actually
make him do it, right? He was willing,
that's all that mattered. A father's love
gave way to dread of Me,
and man, it felt good, real good!

RAIN

The rain's my friend.
It cleans, it dances
on the roof. It says,
"There there, now,
don't you cry,
your poor heart's broke
but it won't die,
not yet. It hears
the pitter patter
of the rain, and knows
the sun will shine again,
some day. And at
the final rain, you'll
smile to see
the human stain
washed clean away
by lovely rain."

BENNY

He talks incessantly, although
of words he has but one, meow,
or two, if we count the yowl,
as we should, because the yowl,
which comes in the middle of the night,
is a whole Russian novel.
Always a handsome fellow,
milky Siamese beige,
with chocolate face, tail, and paws,
he could leap to the top
of the bookcase to a hi-fi speaker
to a lap in the armchair
without missing a beat.
But now, if he were human,
we'd put him in a wheelchair
and swaddle him in adult diapers.
His hind legs don't work right,
he falls over backwards trying
to jump to a couch or a lap,
and today, trying to stand
after a back fall,

he fell over again, sideways.
He's near the end of his ninth life,
but he doesn't know it.
I watch him lick the ice cream
left in my bowl. He's happy.
When he lies beside me
in the armchair, it's like
it's all he's ever wanted.